THE THREE BEARS

Retold by Carol North • illustrated by Lisa McCue

A GOLDEN BOOK • NEW YORK

Western Publishing Company, Inc., Racine, Wisconsin 53404

Once upon a time there were three bears. The father bear was great big, the mother bear was middle-sized, and the baby bear was wee little.

One morning the mother bear made some porridge for breakfast.

She filled a great big bowl for the father bear, a middle-sized bowl for herself, and a wee little bowl for the baby bear.

While the porridge was cooling, the
bears went out for a walk in the woods.

While they were gone, a little girl
named Goldilocks came to their house and
knocked on the door. No one answered,
so she went right in.

Goldilocks saw the three bowls on the table. The porridge smelled so good she decided to taste it.

First she tasted the porridge in the great big bowl. It was too hot.

Next she tasted the porridge in the middle-sized bowl. It was too cold.

Then she tasted the porridge in the wee little bowl and it was just right. So she gobbled it all up.

Goldilocks saw three chairs in the living room.

She sat in the great big chair. It was too hard.

Next she sat in the middle-sized chair. It was too soft.

Then she sat in the wee little chair and
it was just right, but it broke as she sat down.
"Oh, dear!" said Goldilocks.

Goldilocks went upstairs and found three beds. She was tired after her walk in the woods so she decided to take a nap.

First she lay down on the great big bed.
It was too hard.

Next she tried the middle-sized bed. It was
too soft.

Then she lay
down on the wee
little bed and it was
just right. She closed
her eyes and soon
she was fast asleep.

A little while later,
the three bears came back to
the house. They could tell that
someone had been there.

"Someone has been tasting my porridge," said the father bear in his great big voice.

"Someone has been tasting my porridge," said the mother bear in her middle-sized voice.

"And someone has been tasting my porridge and has eaten it all up!" cried the baby bear in his wee little voice.

The three bears went into the living room.

"Someone has been sitting in my chair," said the father bear.

"Someone has been sitting in my chair," said the mother bear.

"And someone has been sitting in my chair and has broken it all to pieces!" cried the baby bear.

Then the three bears went upstairs.
"Someone has been sleeping in my bed," said
the father bear.

"Someone has been sleeping in my bed," said the mother bear.

"And someone has been sleeping in my bed
and she's still here!" cried the baby bear.

Goldilocks opened her eyes and saw the three
bears standing over her.

"Oh, dear," Goldilocks said. She jumped out
of the bed and ran downstairs and out the door.

The three bears watched Goldilocks run away from the house as fast as she could run. They never saw her again because never again did she go for a walk in the woods.